THiS BOOK BELONGS TO:

That's Coola, Tallulah!

That's Coola, Tallulah!

written by Cheryl Chase

illustrated by Giulia Iacopini

About the Author

Cheryl Chase is known throughout the world for being the award-winning voice of Angelica Pickles of the globally popular animated show Rugrats on Nickelodeon. She has received countless fan mail from Paris, Texas to Paris, France. Cheryl lives in Los Angeles. She is a rabbit enthusiast and loves kayaking and writing weekends at the Hotel Del Coronado. To learn more about Cheryl, please visit www.cherylchasebooks.com.

About the Illustrator

Giulia Iacopini is an Italian illustrator currently living in Ireland, where she is working as a background painter for a children's animated series. She loves colors and being able to tell stories through her drawings.

In her free time, Giulia loves to practice sports (almost any kind, but especially kickboxing!), reading, watching musicals and traveling all over the world.

She loves animals — most of all, her black Lab, Napoleone.

To learn more about Giulia's work, you can visit her website at https://www.giuliaiacopini.net.

For my late mother, Stella Hudock.
Thank you for all the sweet support you've given me.
You are the wind beneath my wings always and forever...
- C.C.

For my best friend, always and forever.
I love you, Napo.
- G. I.

I'm Tallulah.

This is Stella Bella.

We are best friends.

One day Stella Bella's mommy said,
"You'll have to play inside today, Stella Bella."

"Tallulah, what do you want to play?" Stella Bella asked.

"Hey, you know what would be fun?" I said.

"Let's color our faces pretty like fairy princesses.
I know where the best face paint is."

"That's coola, Tallulah!" Stella Bella said.

Stella Bella painted our cheeks the pinkiest pink
and our lips the rosiest red.
We were the prettiest fairy princesses that
ever princessed in the whole world.

"Tallulah," said Stella Bella. "I feel bad.
We're messing in Mommy's makeup.
Mommy won't like this."

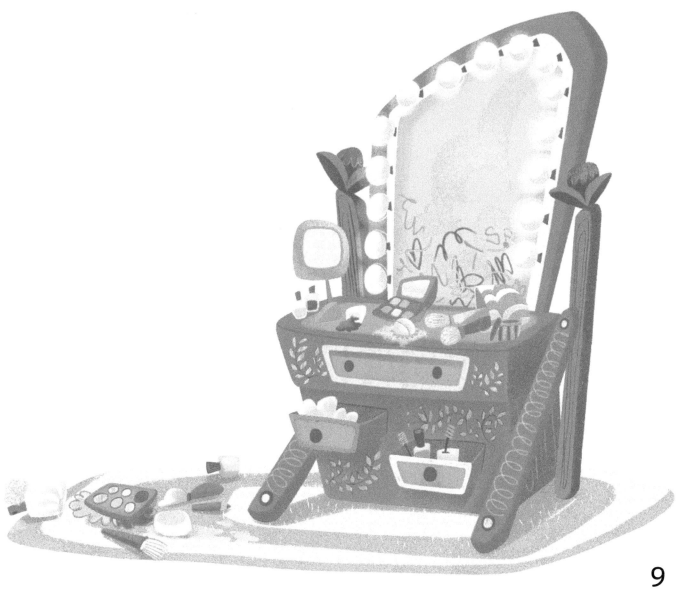

Stella Bella scrubbed
and scrubbed
and scrubbed
and scrubbed.

10

"All clean!" Stella Bella said.
"Let's color instead."

At the art table, I said to Stella Bella,
"Hey, you know what would be fun?
Let's color unicorns!
I know where the best place to color is."

"That's coola,
Tallulah!"

Stella Bella took out our favorite paints
and we made the most unicorny unicorns.

16

"Tallulah," said Stella Bella.
"I feel bad.
We're messing up the walls.
Mommy won't like this."

Stella Bella scrubbed
and scrubbed
and scrubbed
and scrubbed.

18

"All gone!
Now let's have a tea party instead."

At the tea party, I said to Stella Bella, "Hey, you know what would be fun? Let's serve cookies to our guests."

21

Stella Bella pushed the chair
to the counter and climbed up.
She stretched the stretchiest stretch anyone ever
streeeeeeeeeetched!

"Oh my," Stella Bella's mommy said.
"Climbing up to get cookies? No, Stella Bella.
Ask Mommy first. Let's give you a break."

Stella Bella and I are best friends.
When she gets a break, I get a break. So, I got a break.
Stella Bella's mommy put me back on the toy shelf.

"Did I do something wrong?" I asked.
"Yes, you did do something wrong,"
Ricky Robot said.
"You told Stella Bella to get cookies and
she broke the cookie jar," Binky Bunny said.

"That was not a great idea, Tallulah,"
Timmy Tugboat tooted.
"Gee, I only wanted to have fun."
Now I felt sad. I love Stella Bella with all my heart.
I didn't mean to do wrong.

"Tallulah,"
Stella Bella called out.

"Oh, Stella Bella,
I don't want to be apart
from you ever,
ever again!" I cried.

28

"I don't want to be apart from you either, Tallulah.
You're my favorite lovey!
Let's go play on the swings," Stella Bella said.
"Great idea…and I know the swingiest swings!" Tallulah said.
"That's coola, Tallulah!" said Stella Bella.
"And, I've got another great idea, too."

"That's swella,
Stella Bella!"

31

32

CPSIA information can be obtained
at www.ICGtesting.com
Printed in the USA
LVHW071615250622
722125LV00016B/50